ALSO BY THE AUTHOR:

For ages 9+

The Fox Girl and the White Gazelle
Floris Books (April 2018)

The Boy with the Butterfly Mind   Floris Books (Sept 2019)

Stay at Home! Poetry and Prose for Children in Lockdown
Cranachan Publishing (May 2020)

Hag Storm: The Adventures of Robert Burns Book 1
Cranachan Publishing (Oct 2021)

Storm Trackers: Career Book Series
Ignite Hubs (Charity) (Nov 2022)

The Pawnshop of Stolen Dreams
Tiny Tree Publishing (April 2023)

For ages 12+

War of the Wind   Neem Tree Press (Sept 2022)

THE
HAUNTING
SCENT
OF
POPPIES

Little Thorn Books Ltd
1 Quality Court,
Chancery Lane
London
WC2A 1HR

For all enquiries, please email: hello@littlethornbooks.com
www.littlethornbooks.com

Printed in Great Britain

THE
HAUNTING
SCENT
OF
POPPIES

A Ghost Story

VICTORIA WILLIAMSON

little
thorn
books

It was the books that Charlie smelled first – the books that drew him in.

Charlie Briggs had a nose for business, and he wasn't about to let a little thing like the "closed for lunch" sign hanging on the door of the bookshop get between him and a chance to make some unearned cash. He'd already tried his luck with the collection boxes in the church on the opposite side of The Square, but the deacon lighting the candles to commemorate the town's War dead had been standing too close for Charlie to risk forcing their lids. He'd strolled out to the cemetery instead, pretending to pay his respects at the grave of a young soldier to avoid the suspicious gaze of the verger who was struggling to break the frigid ground with his spade. The stone read:

In Loving Memory of Arthur Richards
1896-1917

Huh, Charlie thought as he walked off in search of better opportunities. *Another young fool who barely made it to twenty-one.* As far as he was concerned, now that the War had been officially over for six weeks, it was ancient history. He was willing to bet the shopkeepers and farmers hurrying across The Square to the George Inn were thinking more of hot lunches and pints than the long tragedy that had so recently ended. The military statue of William III glared down at them from his horse, looking less than pleased at being frozen in lead in the middle of Petersfield while its citizens escaped to the warm fires of the Inn.

Charlie knew how the statue felt. He wasn't exactly thrilled at being stuck in a small town this close to Christmas Eve, outside the hustle and bustle of London. But despite the frost nipping the Thames, the City was too hot for him right now. He was wanted by the police for everything from jewellery theft in Mayfair to black market trading in Bethnal

Green. Better to lie low in this small Hampshire town and keep his fingers off anything that had to be fenced through his dealers until things cooled down.

The long list of out-of-bounds items didn't include books, though. Scotland Yard never took book thefts seriously, not unless anyone was mad enough to make a play for one of the little treasures destined for Sotheby's. Charlie might be greedy, but he wasn't stupid. A rare book or two that he could offload in the backrooms of Charing Cross was all he needed to make this temporary exile worthwhile. The bookshop on The Square was the perfect place to find a hidden gem.

His first task was to get inside. This time it wouldn't be hard; he didn't plan on anything more complicated than stepping through the open front door. Lunchtime was the perfect opportunity for a bookshop thief. With no other customers and the eyes of the owner distracted by a plate of sandwiches or a bowl of soup, he could have a couple of rare volumes tucked away in his coat before he'd even finished making pleasantries about the chilly weather. He wouldn't be turned away even if it was lunchtime, he knew that for a fact. Booksellers were too polite as a rule and their profit margins too slim to afford putting a customer off for the price of consuming a slice of ham on rye in peace.

The corners of Charlie's mouth turned up in a toothy grin, giving his weak chin an even more ferret-like appearance than usual. This was going to be too easy.

He rapped smartly on the door of Number One, The Square, the heavy rings on his bony fingers leaving scratch marks on the paintwork. A few moments later, a young woman's face appeared in the window. Charlie watched her size him up, taking in his short, skinny frame, his beady eyes and the way his greedy fingers grasped at the door handle, before she pointed emphatically at the "closed for lunch" sign.

Charlie's grin grew wider, but he covered it with a feigned frown and a sigh of impatience. He loved this part of the game. It wasn't as thrilling as a midnight break-in or a moonlit stroll across the London rooftops trying for unlocked windows, but tricking people into trusting him was fun nonetheless.

With the young woman still eyeing him disapprovingly, he took a gold fob watch from his pocket and checked the time, making sure he held it close enough to the window for her to see the tiny diamonds glittering in its casing. This little beauty was the jackpot he'd hit on his last job, but he didn't have a chance to find a buyer before the police were on his trail and he'd jumped on the last train to nowhere the night before. It might be a little flashy for a man trying to lie low, but nothing screamed "trustworthy wealth" as loud as gold and precious stones.

Charlie watched the young woman's eyes widen as she took a closer look, this time noticing the sharp cut of his Savile Row suit, the expensive Bond Street bowler covering his greasy hair and the glitter of rings on his twitching fingers. She didn't smile, but she did unlock the door and welcome him in.

It worked like a charm.

The smell of books came wafting from every corner of the shop. The sweet musk of old volumes lovingly bound in soft leather. The inky tang of freshly printed hardbacks, their spines rigid and their pages still crisp. It drifted down narrow aisles between the tall shelves, hung in heavy clouds over the bargain table by the window, and curled up like smoke from the clutter of newly acquired stock piled on the counter. Charlie breathed it in eagerly. He was going to find something exciting in here, he could *feel* it.

His pulse quickened, his eyes darting to the glass cabinet by the back wall that held the shop's rarest books. Before he could take another step, the young assistant, eager to help now that she'd sized up his worth, began peppering him with questions.

"Would you like to see our Dickens collection, sir?" she asked, her voice sweet as warm honey as she tried to tempt him into parting with his cash. "We have some lovely first editions. Or how about something older – Scott or Defoe perhaps? If poetry's more to your taste we have a wide selection with beautiful bindings, but if you'd prefer something more modern we have all the latest books from London. Did you serve, sir? We also have a very fine military collection spanning several centuries."

At the mention of the Great War, Charlie winced, but he was professional enough not to let the fixed grin slip from his face. Before he could trot out his rehearsed reply, a disembodied voice said from somewhere behind the counter, "Mary, go and fetch that requisition list I asked you for half an hour ago. I'll be out this afternoon and I'll need you to update it while I'm gone."

"Sorry sir, I forgot." Mary hurried into the shop's backrooms, and Charlie breathed a sigh of relief. This was going to be much easier without an overeager audience watching his every move.

"My assistant, Mary," the voice from behind the stack of books on the counter said by way of explanation. "She's new." Charlie wasn't sure if this was an apology for Mary's overenthusiasm or a rebuke for letting him in during the lunch hour.

"Doctor Harry Roberts." A hand shot out from between the piles of books to shake Charlie's.

"Though you might say I'm new myself – just opened the shop this year."

"Raymond Norris," Charlie lied, smiling at the owner who was seated behind the counter munching on a sandwich. Charlie was amused to see that it was indeed ham on rye. "Pleased to meet you."

"Been wanting to open my own bookshop for a while now, but I had to do my duty for King and country first," Doctor Roberts said through a mouthful of bread. "Lost a lot of good lads from Petersfield. We're having a bit of a collection towards a cenotaph…" He waved his crust in the direction of the jar of coins on the counter. Charlie felt obligated to dig into his pockets and pull out a handful of low-denomination coins.

"Much obliged," Doctor Roberts smiled.

"Not at all, my pleasure," Charlie smiled back as he secretly palmed the rare gold sovereign he'd spied near the top of the jar with expert fingers. It felt satisfyingly heavy in his waistcoat pocket, and a familiar greedy thrill tingled up his spine.

"It's important we remember them, the sacrifice they made. That we all made," Doctor Roberts said, gazing off into the distance as though lost in his own sad memories of that terrible time. He shook his head, then looked Charlie up and down for the first time. "Serve yourself, did you?"

Charlie glanced at the framed photo on the wall behind the counter, of Doctor Roberts in uniform surrounded by a group of grinning soldiers. In under three seconds he'd sized up their insignia, figured out their regiment was the Hampshire, and picked a backstory the good doctor would never be able to verify.

"South Staffordshire – got this at the second battle of Passchendaele," Charlie rattled off, moving his stiff collar slightly so the doctor could see the tail end of the long scar that snaked from his neck right down to his navel.

"Gosh, that's some blighty! Brave chap," the Doctor nodded approvingly.

Charlie grinned back, fighting the urge to laugh. He'd got his "war wound" falling out of a window when a job went wrong in Highgate, but it would never do to tell the truth to an upstanding gentleman like Doctor Roberts. The truth was Charlie hadn't so much as set foot in France, never mind seen a single day of service. When his draft papers came early in 1915 he'd paid a corrupt surgeon to sign him off as unfit for duty with weak lungs, and he'd spent the War merrily stealing his way round London, hoarding limited food supplies and selling them to the highest bidder on the black market. The war years had been some of the best of his life.

He was just about to leave the Doctor to his sandwich and explore the treasures on the shelves, when his eyes came to rest on a book on the counter, the one the Doctor had been reading when Charlie came in. It was closed now, and Charlie could read the title on the faded cover:

Art Militaire Des Chinois, Ou Recueil D'Anciens Traites Sur La Guerre.

Charlie might never have seen action in Ypres or be able to order a pint in French, but he knew the title of every rare book on his buyer's most-wanted list and could reel them all off in every language. At the top of this list was the 1772 first edition sitting in front of him. No matter how many bookshops he'd trawled, *The Art of War* by Sun Tzu had always eluded him. Now here it was, right within his grasp. All he had to do was reach out a hand and…

"Interested in military history, are you?" Doctor Roberts must have seen a change in Charlie's expression, something he didn't like. He moved the book just a little further away and took a key from his pocket. Charlie had enough experience with safe keys to know he was one step away from seeing his prize locked out of easy reach. He didn't want to return for a night-time break-in to retrieve it, that was too risky, so he said quickly, "No, not my line at all. I've seen more than enough battles to last me a lifetime, as I'm sure you'll understand."

The Doctor nodded, his face relaxing.

"And embarrassing though it is to admit, I can barely speak a word of French after all those years – just don't have the head for it," Charlie said smoothly.

The Doctor's smile returned, and he put the safe key down on top of the book and picked up his sandwich again.

"Think I'll take a look at the poetry – that's more my thing. Don't mind me, though, I'm disturbing your luncheon, and your reading. Good book, is it?"

Charlie's fishing was rewarded by the Doctor taking a big bite of his hook. "It's a real treasure this one," the Doctor nodded. "Never thought I'd see one in the flesh, as it were. It's not for sale, though," he added quickly, "it was a gift. Well, more of a legacy. Sad story, it belonged to a young lad from round here who died in the trenches. His mother was one of my closest friends, and..." the Doctor trailed off, the distant look in his eyes returning. "It doesn't matter now," he sighed and repeated, "but it's not for sale."

"Of course, not my line anyway, as I said." Charlie didn't want the finger of blame pointing anywhere near him once the little book had vanished into his coat pocket. "I'll just be over here browsing your poetry shelves."

"Take your time. I must dash out, I have some art prints to look over this afternoon. Mary will take care of anything you need. Mary?" he called, just as the young assistant was re-emerging from the backrooms clutching a pile of papers. "Ah Mary, there you are. Help this gentleman with anything he requires – I promised Flora I'd go and look at her pictures. Put my book away in the safe for me, will you? And make sure those requisition lists are completed and posted by the time you close up. I won't be back in the shop again until we're open in the New Year."

Dr Roberts pulled on his jacket, grabbed the last of his sandwich, and gave Charlie a friendly nod as he hurried out of the shop, leaving Mary hesitating between the stack of papers in her hand, the customer by the shelves, and the rare book lying on the counter.

Charlie seized his chance to make her mind up for her.

"I was very interested in this Keats collection," he said, taking a book from the shelf and showing it to her, "but I'm a bit disappointed by the binding. I don't know much about these things, but it's a gift for a friend, and she does love her books to look nice."

"We keep the finer bindings in the back. I'll go and fetch what we have for you to look through."

As soon as Mary disappeared into the storerooms again, Charlie was back at the counter, his greedy hand reaching out for *The Art of War*. Just as his fingers closed over the old brown leather, he felt a stinging pain shooting up his arm all the way to his shoulder. For a moment it felt almost as though the pages were made of nettles instead of paper. He dropped the book with a thump, the safe key rattling on the countertop.

"Everything alright, sir?" Mary's voice called from the backroom.

"Fine, fine," Charlie called back breezily, cursing himself. He was getting too eager. This had to be done properly. He skimmed the shelves quickly, looking for a book with the same marbled brown leather as his target, with similar tooling on the spine. Selecting one of roughly the same size, he hurried back to the counter and switched the books out, lifting *The Art of War* gingerly by its edges and hiding it deep inside his coat, turning the replacement so its spine was facing away from Mary with the key on top. He could only hope she was too distracted to check the title before she put it away in the safe.

When she came back with a small pile of books, Charlie made a big show of examining them carefully before selecting a little volume with a handsome red leather cover. It was not so expensive that it would eat into his emergency escape fund, but rich enough that it would buy him some measure of protection from suspicion. Genuine, respectable bookshop customers bought books, and Charlie needed to be remembered as polite and trustworthy when the Doctor's treasure was discovered missing.

Switching the books out had been the easy bit. Now came the hard part, the part that might require what Charlie called 'rough work'. He didn't like the word 'violence'. He didn't like to think of himself as a brutal man, just one who was willing to do what had to be done. He paid Mary for the book, tipped his hat with a smile and walked out of the door with his legitimately purchased book under his arm and his stolen prize hidden under his coat. He only walked five steps to the corner, then stopped to peer into the bookshop window, watching to see what Mary would do next.

The next ten seconds would seal her fate.

Mary picked the substituted book up from the counter. Charlie's eyes narrowed, his fingers playing with the long, fine piece of wire he kept in his pocket for emergencies. He didn't like to use it, but sometimes people needed to be silenced. He watched carefully to see if the bookshop assistant would be one of them.

Mary didn't turn the book over. She glanced at the front door as though remembering something, then hurried over to lock it again, making sure the "closed for lunch" sign was still in place. She straightened some volumes on the bargain table, ran her finger along one of the tall shelves to check for dust, and finally took the replacement book to the backroom, disappearing from view. Charlie counted to twenty slowly, then edged towards the door. She was taking too long. She must have discovered the switch. The hand in his pocket closed over the piano wire, the other hand taking out a set of lock picks.

Mary reappeared again just as he was about to insert a small file into the keyhole. Her own hands were empty, and she cleared the piles of books from the counter, sitting down with the requisition forms and setting to work. She didn't look as though she'd discovered a terrible crime had been committed. She just looked bored.

Charlie grinned. He'd got away with it. Mary would close the shop up tonight and the Doctor wouldn't return to open the safe until the New Year, by which time Charlie and the book would be long gone. It felt strangely heavy against his chest for such a small volume, and for a moment he felt his breath catch in his lungs, almost as though the pressure was choking him. He staggered, leaning against the wall and clutching at his throat, trying to loosen his tight collar.

A passerby threw him a strange look, and Charlie turned his face away, drawing his bowler hat further down to shield his eyes. Lunchtime was almost over, and the shops were beginning to open their doors. Soon the streets would be full again, and Charlie didn't want to be spotted anywhere near the bookshop, just in case.

The choking feeling passed, and now that he'd got away with his crime he felt strangely lightheaded – so light he could float down the street if his boots weren't anchoring him firmly to the road. His stomach rumbled, and he rubbed his woozy head, glad the dizzy spell was nothing more than a reminder that he had yet to have lunch himself.

There was one more job to do before he could celebrate with a steak pie and a well-earned pint of ale, though. He set off down Chapel Street, heading for the Post Office on the corner of Levant Street, which he had passed on his way from the train station the night before. He needed to call Keeler, his most trusted dealer, to tell him the good news. Keeler would know what to do with the book. For the right price he'd find a buyer for both the book and the glittering fob watch burning a hole in his waistcoat pocket, and Charlie would have the funds he so badly needed to stay hidden away from London as long as he needed.

This was his lucky day. Everything had gone right for him since he arrived in this little backwater town. His grin grew wider. Perhaps he'd stop in Petersfield longer than he'd been planning.

* * * * * *

By the time Charlie had made his telephone call and returned to the Spain Arms where he was renting a room, he'd changed his mind about staying any longer in Petersfield. He'd chosen this public house because it was cheap, and the steady stream of labourers passing through looking for work wouldn't pay too much attention to a thief like him.

But he'd miscalculated. He wasn't in his usual shabby working clothes which helped him blend in.

He chewed his greasy steak pie slowly, sensing the eyes of the other men in the public house watching him. They didn't see the real Charlie Briggs, the one who hid in the shadows and went hungry between jobs. He'd never had enough willpower to stay away from the gaming tables for long. His money was no sooner earned than it vanished on the turn of a card or the roll of a dice. This was the first hot meal he'd had in five days.

They didn't see any of that. All they saw was his expensive suit and bowler, and the gold chain pointing to the treasure hidden in his waistcoat pocket. They didn't know he'd stolen the lot from the last house he'd burgled. To them he was a mark, the kind of man Charlie himself usually picked out of the crowd to follow into a back alley. He was taking a risk he could ill afford by staying here.

He swallowed hastily, downing the last of his ale and retreating to his room. He shouldn't have been so quick to choose this as his hiding place last night. He should have looked around to find a more suitable private guest house until the heat in London died down, even if it meant using up the last of his funds.

He'd remedy that mistake right now.

Charlie took his small travelling bag out from under his bed, grabbing his razor from the chipped bowl on the washstand and pinching a towel from the rail to wrap it in. Besides the small blade that doubled as a weapon, a change of shirt, a comb, and a couple of cigarettes left in a crumpled packet were the sum total of all his worldly goods.

Were the sum total, Charlie smiled to himself, his eyes roving over his fine suit, the gold watch chain, and the bulge of the book in his coat that were going to earn his fortune. Once they were sold and he'd got his cut from Keeler, his worries would be over for the foreseeable future. Maybe he'd even set himself up as a dealer like Keeler, instead of a common thief.

Charlie Briggs, the respectable gentleman, think of that! he chuckled.

He knew he should get out right there and then. The eyes in the bar below had been too keen, too searching. But the book was calling to him, and he couldn't resist a closer look.

His expensive coat was hanging over the back of a chair, and Charlie gingerly drew the small leather book from the inside pocket, remembering the awful sting he'd felt the last time he'd touched it. It felt cool and heavy in his hands now, and Charlie was relieved to be able to tell himself the strange burning sensation in the bookshop had just been a muscle twinge. He wasn't as young as he used to be – yet another reason why he needed one last big payout to get out of the game while he still could.

Opening the book, his fingers traced the inscription on the inside page. It was slightly faded now, as though other fingers, perhaps more loving than his, had been in the habit of touching the words that said:

To my darling son, Arthur, on his eighteenth birthday.

This book was the jewel in your father's collection, and despite my disapproval of its subject matter, I know he would be proud to see it passed on to you. I give this to you to encourage your love of reading and remind you of your dream to open your own bookshop.

With all my love, your affectionate mother, Ruth Richards.

Petersfield, 3rd August 1914.

One day before the start of the War, Charlie thought to himself. *What a day to turn eighteen.*

He turned over the pages slowly, and was excited to see they were in pristine condition despite the age of the book. That would definitely make up for the silly woman devaluing the rare volume with her own worthless birthday sentiments.

Turning over another page, something red caught Charlie's eye, and for a moment his heart missed a beat. If it was a stain, his retirement plan might have to wait a few more years yet. Taking a closer look, he was relieved to find it was a dried flower that had perhaps been used as a bookmark. What a stupid thing to put between the pages of such a rare book. Luckily it hadn't left a mark.

Charlie carefully pulled out the poppy, making sure the dried petals didn't crumble as he removed it. It gave off a faint odour, of something sickly sweet and yet bitter at the same time. He wrinkled his nose in disgust and threw the poppy onto the small fire the landlord had grudgingly lit for him. At once the flames leapt up. The acrid smell grew stronger, filling the whole room until Charlie's head was reeling and he was gasping for breath. He made a desperate lunge for the door, but his feet refused to follow, and he found himself falling backwards onto the chair that seemed to rise up from the floor to catch him. The room spun and then began to recede, lost in a mustard-coloured cloud that hung heavy with the rich scent of opium.

Charlie's eyes closed. The book slipped from his lap, and he dreamed.

Charlie had never seen hell, but he knew that's where he was now. The darkness swallowed him whole, flaring brightly every few moments as bursts of fire cut the air like lightning. At first the silence roared so loud in his ears he thought he must have gone deaf. Then another bone-shaking explosion sent huge mounds of dirt flying in every direction, and he realised his eardrums were still recovering from the shock of the last blast. His feet were icy cold, thick mud sucking at his boots as he slipped and slithered through a deep trench.

He wasn't alone. All around him men in blood-spattered uniforms were yelling themselves hoarse over the pounding noise of shell-fire, their guns rattling back a weak response to the overwhelming onslaught. Another explosion sent Charlie crashing to his knees, spattering the wooden walls trapping him with blood. The three soldiers nearest him had perished, and shreds of uniform and a few grisly remains were all that was left in the churned-up mud.

Charlie whimpered in fear, hunkering down in the freezing muck and shielding his head with his arms.

This isn't real, he told himself over and over. *You were never here!*

A new cry split the air, uttering one nightmare word so awful it rang like the toll of a death bell for every poor wretch who heard it.

"Gas!" a voice screamed. "*GAS!*"

Charlie stumbled to his feet again, twisting and turning, not knowing which direction to run.

"Get to higher ground!" another voice yelled in his ear. "It's pooling down here – be quick!"

Charlie's whole body was frozen in shock, and he stared dumbly at the young man who tried to shove him into action.

"Gas?" he spluttered, not understanding. "Pooling?"

"It's mustard gas, you fool! Don't you know anything? Climb, man! Climb!"

His rescuer pushed him towards a ladder attached to the trench wall, and Charlie grasped the rungs with shaking hands, pulling himself up towards the sounds of heavy gunfire despite his instincts screaming at him to stay cowering in the trench.

Another shell exploded nearby, shaking the wall so hard Charlie nearly let go of the ladder. As the light flared again, he looked round just in time to see the young man who'd saved him pitching backwards through the gas cloud into a toxic bath of contaminated mud. The bitter-smelling liquid closed over the soldier's head in a baptism of fire, and Charlie shuddered at the thought of what that burning pool would do to the young man's flesh.

The young man's head re-emerged, his hands scrabbling at the trench walls, trying to find enough purchase to pull himself out.

"Help me!" he croaked. "Help!"

He reached a hand up towards Charlie, who hesitated on the ladder for a long moment. If he leaned back now he could fall, and the soldier was already soaked through with whatever was down there.

He's a goner, Charlie told himself, turning away. *Not my problem.*

Just two more rungs and he'd be out in the open, away from the awful stench that made him retch. As his hands reached for the last rung, something shifted in his coat, and he felt a weight slip from his inside pocket.

The book! Charlie realised with a start. *I must save the book!*

He snatched at it as it fell, but the cover slipped through his fingers, tumbling down into the pool of mud and gas below. Charlie scrambled back a few rungs, stretching out for it before it sank. For a moment the floundering soldier thought Charlie had come back for him.

"Help me!" he coughed again, "I can't get out! Help me!"

Charlie saw the hope in the young man's blistered face change to a look of despair as he realised it was greed, not mercy, that had made Charlie turn back. As Charlie's grasping fingers reached out for the sinking book, the young soldier's plea for help changed, and he spat out, *"Remember me."*

It sounded like a curse.

Charlie lost his grip on the ladder and went tumbling headfirst down into the sulphurous fog.

He woke with a start, gasping for breath and thrashing his arms.

"Remember me."

The words seemed to hang on the air, collecting in the dark corners and pooling in the cracks between the floorboards. Charlie shivered. The fire had long gone out and twilight had fallen. The cloying smell had faded, and now only a faint trace of mustard lingered as a bitter aftertaste. He rubbed his eyes. They were sore and itching, as though he'd been scratching them in his sleep. His hands were stinging too, a burning sensation that flared all the way up from his fingertips to his wrists.

Charlie blinked hard, trying to bring the blurry world back into focus again. The first thing he saw when his vision cleared and he looked at his hands were the red blotches that covered his skin. That wasn't what made his heart pound though. It was what he *didn't* see that made his stomach lurch.

His rings were gone. All of them.

In one swift motion, he ran his hands across his chest and checked his waistcoat pockets. His fob watch was gone too, and his pilfered gold sovereign. He leapt to his feet, reaching for his expensive coat to check its pockets. It had vanished, and hanging in its place on the back of the chair was a shabby working jacket, the kind a day labourer would wear. Charlie picked it up and turned it over, before throwing it back down again in disgust.

His travelling bag had been rifled through, and his razor and spare shirt taken. Even the bowler hat and book of poetry he'd left on the small table had been stolen.

The book!

Charlie stumbled around the room in alarm, looking for the precious volume he couldn't afford to lose. After a few moments of panic-stricken searching, he let out a sigh of relief, finding it tucked under his chair where it had fallen. The thieves must have missed it when they ransacked his room.

Charlie sank down on the chair again, his mind racing. Somehow, he must have been drugged by some of the customers who'd been watching him at lunch. Perhaps they'd slipped something into his ale, or maybe there was something put into his fire that sent him to sleep and left his skin itching like the very devil. Yes! That was it. Just before he fell into that nightmare the air had become heavy and he'd struggled to breathe. They must have tampered with the coals. But the landlord laid the fire himself – that must mean he was in on it too.

Charlie weighed up his limited options. He couldn't report the theft to the police, that was certain, not when half of Scotland Yard was looking for him. He could try hunting the thieves down, but if they were smart, they would already have vanished. If he asked downstairs, no one would admit to seeing anything. He'd been a fool to stay here with such a rich cache of goods, a stupid, amateur fool, and now he was paying for it. His only consolation was he hadn't lost his real prize, and his book was still safe.

There was only one option open to him now, and that was to find a safer guest house for the next few days.

Charlie checked his trouser pockets, and was relieved to find there were still a few coins left there. Enough to buy a roof over his head for tonight at any rate. He gathered up what was left of his possessions, shrugged on the tattered jacket that was too small even for his skinny frame, and headed down the back stairs before slipping out into the night.

* * * * *

"Did you sleep alright, Mr Harrison?"

"Hmph?" For a moment Charlie forgot the fake name he'd given the landlady the night before. "Oh yes, very well, Miss Richards, thank you."

It was another lie. Although his room in the little guest house tucked away in a corner of St Peter's Road was very comfortable, he'd tossed and turned all night, plagued by the strange dream of the trenches and the young man trapped in the pool of sulphurous mustard. His hands were itching badly this morning, and small blisters had broken out across them, making it painful for him to lift his teacup. He smiled at the landlady across the breakfast table though, despite his bloodshot eyes and itching skin. He couldn't afford to arouse any more suspicion.

She'd been reluctant to let him over the threshold when he'd turned up on her doorstep last night, out of breath and more dishevelled than usual. He couldn't blame her. With his shabby labourer's coat and wild look in his eyes, he was a far cry from the respectable gentleman in the fine suit who'd stepped off the train the previous evening. The fear in his eyes hadn't been his fault, though.

No. That had been... something else.

All the way up Sheep Street, he'd had the disconcerting feeling that something was following him. Whenever he'd turned to look back he'd caught faint glimpses of a figure lurking in the shadows behind him. It had a shambling gait, but it limped and hobbled with surprising speed from one dark corner to the next, never quite coming into full view.

At first Charlie had thought one of the labourers from the Spain Arms was following him, watching to see if he was heading for the police station to report the theft. But by the time he'd reached The Square, he knew it was something else. Something hunched and twisted, swathed in loose bandages that trailed and flapped in the breeze. In the darkness it has seemed as though there was no face to it, only two round hollows for eyes that glowed red in the darkness like hot coals. He knew that was just his imagination playing tricks on him after his nightmare, but that didn't stop him quickening his pace to escape the uncanny sight.

Charlie had always prided himself on his nerves of steel, but last night he'd nearly screamed out loud when he'd turned back at St Peter's Church and seen the thing shambling through the cemetery towards him. He'd clutched his travelling bag containing the rare book tighter, breaking into a run down St Peter's Road and pounding on the door of the first guest house he'd come to. Luckily Miss Richards had believed his story of being newly arrived and robbed on the train, or his hallucination would have caught up with him.

He'd looked over his shoulder when she ushered him in, but it was nowhere to be seen, fading back into the night as though it had never been there at all.

Pull yourself together, Charlie! He told himself. *You've just overworked yourself these last few days, what with the Berkeley Square break-in and the last-minute dash from London. A week or so of peace and quiet here, and Keeler will have the book deal set up. You can go back to the City, collect your cash, and leave this awful little town behind you.*

As for his itching skin, he put that down to whatever the thieves at the Spain Arms had drugged him with before they robbed him.

"More tea, Mr Harrison?" The elderly landlady shuffled back into the breakfast room with a fresh pot, setting down a plate of hot toast. He was the only guest this late in the year, and it had taken all of his charm to persuade her to let him stay over Christmas, despite the fact that she had no family of her own.

"Thank you, Miss Richards, you're too kind." He smiled at her, searching the dreary little room for something else to compliment her on to keep her sweet. He had only enough money to pay one more night up front, so he'd need to ensure she trusted him to settle the bill when he left. Noticing the overladen bookshelf in the corner, he was about to make a polite comment about her love of literature, when his itching eyes came to rest on the red flowers that were growing in the window box outside on the sill. He'd already said, "What beautiful flowers!" before he realised that poppies at this time of year were unheard of.

"Flowers?" Miss Richards looked round in confusion. "What...? Oh! Those. There's a lovely little shop on Chapel Street that makes them. They cheer everything up in winter, don't they? Even if they are only silk."

"Silk..?" Charlie looked again. The poppies on the sill had vanished, the window box empty except for a few dried weeds. The silk flowers Miss Richards was referring to stood in a vase by the fireplace. He nodded, pretending that was what he had meant, silently cursing the thieves whose strange smoke had interfered with his vision. He was seeing things even in broad daylight now.

"My sister-in-law, Ruth, loved flowers," Miss Richards said, sitting down opposite Charlie at the small table and pouring herself a cup of tea. "She always wanted the house to look its best in case the War ended early and Arthur came home unannounced. I like to keep some flowers in every room so the old place won't forget her."

"This isn't your house then?" Charlie asked. He wasn't really interested in her story, but his blistered hands were itching badly, and keeping her talking was the best way for him to scratch them under the table without her noticing.

"No, it belonged to my brother, John. After he died in the Boer War it passed to Ruth. John had such a passion for collecting books we used to joke he could open his own shop right here in the parlour!" The old woman smiled sadly at the memory. "I just wish his love of reading was the only thing poor Arthur inherited from his father, then perhaps..." She trailed off, staring into her teacup.

Wait a minute! Ruth and Arthur Richards? It was as though spark had flickered to life in his fog-filled brain, and he jumped up eagerly, hurrying over to the bookcase in the corner. *The Art of War* had come from this very collection. There might be more treasures just waiting to be discovered on the shelves.

"Are you interested in books too?" Miss Richards asked as he scanned the titles, searching for something that would fetch more than a few shillings. "You're welcome to borrow any of them during your stay. None of them are particularly valuable, but as they belonged to my dear nephew, I would ask that you treat them carefully."

"Of course," Charlie nodded, hiding his disappointment. "I was just looking to see if there were any books about Petersfield here. It's a very picturesque little town."

"No local histories, I'm afraid. My brother John's taste ran more to military history and biographies, as you can see. Perhaps if Ruth had got rid of the books after he passed, Arthur might not have inherited that particular passion too."

"An interest in the military?"

"And in fighting in a war," Miss Richards sighed. "He wanted to honour the memory of his father, make him proud. He didn't wait a single day when war with Germany was declared, he signed up there and then. Ruth and I couldn't stop him, he'd turned eighteen just the day before. Ruth blamed herself, she thought giving him that last book was what encouraged him, almost as though she'd given him her blessing, but..."

Miss Richards trailed off with a sniff. Charlie waited, trying to look respectfully grave while she dabbed her eyes with a handkerchief and straightened the lacy cap covering her grey hair, but his impatience got the better of him and he prompted, "What book?"

"Oh, a French translation about warfare that belonged to my father, and his grandfather before him. There was some family superstition attached to it, something about its owners dying in battle or some such thing, but in a family where all the men have served, that's hardly surprising, is it?"

Miss Richards stood up to clear the breakfast things away, but Charlie wanted to hear more. A book's provenance could add to its value, and a tasty family mystery might even redeem the stupid inscription that would otherwise devalue it.

"And did they?" he asked, a little too eagerly. "Did the owners of the book all die in battle?"

Miss Richards threw him a searching look, and set down her teacup so hard it rattled in its saucer. "It's all nonsense," she snorted, "just a silly story that was passed down. But Ruth believed it, poor thing. It broke her heart when Arthur died last Christmas Eve. It broke both our hearts."

She picked up a photograph of a dark-haired woman that was sitting on a side table, dabbing her eyes with her handkerchief again as she gazed at it. Charlie knew he'd have to tread a little more carefully.

"And the book?" he asked. "What happened to the book in the end?"

He already knew where it had ended up, but he wanted to know how it had got there.

"I gave it away," Miss Richards sniffed. "I'm not superstitious, but Ruth wouldn't have wanted it kept in the family after what happened to Arthur. And after what she did to herself when he died..." Miss Richards bit her lip, then hurried on, "well, I gave it to Doctor Roberts. He's an old family friend, and he loves books just as much as Arthur did. He was going to take Arthur on at his bookshop after the War, only..."

"You gave away such a rare volume instead of selling it?" Charlie couldn't help asking.

The suspicious look returned to Miss Richards' pinched face, and she pushed her spectacles further up her nose to examine him more carefully. "How did you know that book was particularly rare, Mr Harrison?"

"You said yourself that none of the rest were worth much – I assumed you meant there were a few others in the collection that had value." He smiled breezily, hoping the old lady's spectacles weren't strong enough to see through his lies.

"Oh. Of course. Well, it didn't seem right selling it to a stranger. It was meant to stay in the family, and Doctor Roberts was like an uncle to Arthur, so my poor nephew wouldn't mind him having it. Such a fine boy," she sighed again. "Such a terrible waste."

Charlie turned to look at the picture on the mantelpiece she was gazing at, and his heart skipped a beat. Staring back at him accusingly was the same young man in uniform that he'd seen in his nightmare.

The logs on the fire spluttered. Sparks flew up as the wood shifted and resettled, and just for a moment, it seemed as though the eyes in the picture were glowing red. Instead of the sweet smell of wood smoke, the room seemed to fill with the choking fumes of something stronger. Charlie coughed and clutched at his throat, his lungs suddenly burning.

"Why, Mr Harrison! What on earth is the matter? You look like you've seen a ghost!"

The acrid smell of charred garlic faded away, until only the faint scent of poppies lingered in the stuffy room. "Nothing, Miss Richards, I'm fine," Charlie spluttered. "Still a little shaken up after that incident on the train last night, that's all."

"Of course. I hope the police find those awful thieves. In the meantime, you look like you could do with some fresh air. Why don't you go for a nice walk round the Heath Pond? That'll do you the world of good. You'll have to go the long way round now that the best route's been chained up to make a private road – a bone of contention round here and no mistake – but it's a nice bright day for it."

"I think I'll do that, Miss Richards, thank you." Charlie rubbed his aching eyes and went upstairs to fetch his shabby coat. He wasn't one for pleasure walks, but he needed to get out of the house, away from those too-familiar eyes on the mantelpiece and the strange smell that lingered on the air.

* * * * * *

Charlie had hoped he'd meet with more people on his walk around the Heath Pond. He was safest in a crowd, and right now he could do with some handy pockets to pick.

But despite the chill in the air and the frost that crunched underfoot, the Pond hadn't frozen over, and there was no snow to tempt groups of ice skaters or sledgers away from their Christmas shopping. It was too late in the year for boating parties, and the occasional walkers he passed were gone before he could size them up, rubbing their cold hands and hurrying to finish their morning constitutionals so they could return to their warm fires.

Charlie's own hands were too sore for anything quick and deft now anyway. With the blisters starting to burst and the rash spreading up his arms, his fingers were almost too swollen and cracked to bear putting in his own pockets never mind anyone else's. He cursed the public house thieves for the hundredth time, wondering what on earth it was they'd dosed him with that had caused such a painful reaction.

A small voice at the back of his head was whispering disconcerting words about the book and photograph on the mantelpiece, but Charlie ignored it, focusing instead on the more pressing matter of how to get hold of some ready cash. With the state his hands were in, it wasn't going to be easy. When he got back to the guest house, he'd have to look for something worth pawning, which, going by the faded furnishings and the meagre breakfast he'd been served that morning, wasn't going to be easy either.

He had just made up his mind to search the pokey little kitchen for silver spoons, when something caught his eye. A frail red flower was dancing in the wind, its petals red as blood against the white frost carpeting the grass.

It was a single poppy, growing so far out of season it no longer seemed like a symbol of summer life, but a grotesque warning of death.

Swallowing down the bitter taste of foreboding, Charlie strode over and plucked the flower from its stalk, crushing the petals with his blistered hands.

See? It's just a stupid flower. Nothing to be scared of, he told himself. Red juice oozed between his fingers, and he dropped the pulped remains in disgust. As soon as they hit the ground they seemed to melt into the frost, the flower vanishing as though it had never really been there. Unnerved, Charlie backed away.

That was when he saw it.

Something was moving between the trees that circled the Heath Pond.

Charlie blinked hard, trying to make out more than just a sinister shape in the gloom. The pale sun had disappeared behind thick cloud, and the sky was grey and louring, almost as though the heavens were frowning down on him. His puffy eyes were itching more than ever, refusing to cooperate. All he could say for sure was that the figure was hunched over and shambling along at great speed, and that he'd seen it coming for him the night before.

The path ahead was deserted. Charlie was alone with the figure in the shadows, with the wide expanse of the Heath Pond blocking his escape back to town. The water seemed somehow darker than before, an unnatural yellow mist rising from its surface. The smell of mustard filled the air, and Charlie covered his nose with his sleeve and broke into a jog, his stomach knotting in fear.

What the hell is that thing? He thought, his mind whirling as his boots pounded along the path. *What the hell is going on?*

The stolen book in his coat pocket thumped against his chest as he ran, knocking the air out of his lungs. He couldn't leave it in the guest house in case Miss Richards came across it while she was cleaning and recognised it instantly, but the pocket of his shabby jacket was barely large enough to hold it. He gulped down a big breath of the foul mist and instantly regretted it, coughing and choking on its bitter fumes.

Was this whole town poisoned? Was the water source contaminated and causing all of this?

He didn't have time to work out where the pungent smell was coming from. Looking over his shoulder, he could see the shambling figure was gaining on him, lurching from tree to tree in determined pursuit. Charlie wasn't going to make it. The road back to town was too far away, a long detour skirting the fenced-off private lands.

He would have to do what he always did when he was in a fix. He would have to take a shortcut.

He clambered over a wooden gate that led to a private road, his hands protesting as his blisters rubbed and burst against the rough wood. The fumes from the lake were aggravating the inflammation, and now his neck and face were stinging as though he'd been shaving with a blunt razor. His eyes ached, and he screwed them up, squinting to make out the road ahead. It was a long, straight avenue, with trees growing so close on either side they blocked off any daylight from above. It was dark and unnaturally quiet in that wooded tunnel, but it was a far more direct route to town.

Charlie didn't have a choice.

He set off down the road, curling his hands into fists and forcing his feet on faster. The yellow mist swirled around him, rising from the lake and spreading through the trees in a choking blanket until he could barely see the ground ahead. Sounds became muffled, until all he could hear was the thump of his feet on the gravel path and the pounding of his heart in his chest. His lungs ached, and he was coughing so hard he could barely draw breath. He slowed to a stop, leaning on his knees and trying to shake off the icy fingers of fear that were clawing their way up his spine. He turned to look back, hoping the high fence had been enough of a deterrent to his pursuer.

At first he saw only the skeleton shapes of trees through the mist, their bony branches tangling in a thick canopy overhead. Then he saw something else.

Red eyes in the mist, and a dark shape that came stumbling through the gloom not ten feet from where he stood.

The figure was almost upon him.

Charlie just had time to catch a glimpse of a tattered uniform half hidden under a layer of dirty bandages that trailed in the breeze. Then he was off again, racing down the long avenue as fast as his feet would carry him.

This time he didn't get far.

Rising above him at the end of the road and cutting off his escape was a row of iron railings. A set of gates stood before him, chained together and padlocked shut. The owner of the land clearly did not like trespassers on his private road. Charlie's aching hand reached instinctively for his lock picks, but found only an empty pocket.

Damn! They were in my other coat!

He rattled the gate to test the chain, but it was solid, and the padlock was thick and heavy. Before he had time to think through his options, he heard a gurgling noise behind him, a horrible rasping and rattling as though someone with lungs full of holes was trying to speak. The shuffling on the gravel path grew louder, but Charlie didn't have the nerve to turn his head and look. He lunged for the gate, grabbing at the iron bars and pulling himself up, his hands shrieking with pain and his throat burning with the sulphurous smell of mustard that hung on the air.

Just as his blistered fingers grasped the metal spikes topping the gate, Charlie felt something brush his ankle. He looked back. A burned claw of what had once been a hand was reaching out of the mist for him, pus-covered bandages loosely flapping at the wrist.

Red eyes stared up him. Burning. Accusing.

"Remember me!" a choked voice whispered somewhere in the gloom.

For a moment Charlie was back in the terrible nightmare of the trenches, looking down at the young soldier floundering in the mud.

The ruined hand scrabbled up his leg towards his chest, and Charlie couldn't tell if it was reaching for the book in his pocket or for his neck. Before it could take hold of him he heaved himself up, tearing his trousers and gashing his arm on the spikes at the top of the gate as he tumbled over.

He landed with a thump on the other side, his whole body bruised and battered by the fall. Gasping for breath, he whirled round, his eyes darting wildly right and left, searching for signs of his pursuer.

The mist had vanished, the gravel on the tree-lined avenue glittering in the light of the pale winter sun. The air was fresh and clear, the sharp nip of frost the only scent carried on the breeze. A robin fluttered from a bush onto the road, its song joining that of the crows sheltering in the high branches.

All was calm. All was peaceful.

The figure was gone.

* * * * * *

Charlie's swollen hands were shaking so badly by the time he got back to the guest house he could barely get his key in the lock. Hearing the heavy thumps and scrapes coming from the front door,

Miss Richards hurried through the hall to let him in, her eyes widening when she saw the dishevelled state of her lodger panting on the doorstep.

"Heavens, Mr Harrison! What on earth has happened to you!"

"Tripped on the Pond walk. Tree root or something. Got a little banged up," Charlie gasped. "No need for lunch, Miss Richards. Think I'll just go and have a little lie down."

"Oh, but your poor hands!" Miss Richards caught sight of his blistered, broken skin as he grasped the balustrade. "I'll bring you up something to bathe them in."

"No need," Charlie said quickly, to put her off following him. "I've had a lot worse."

"Yes, of course you have, during the War no doubt. Poor Arthur came back in such a state..."

Being mistaken for a war hero usually made Charlie grin to himself. Now it just turned his stomach. "Speaking of the War, Miss Richards," he forced himself to say, though he didn't really want to hear her answer, "I've been thinking about your nephew. I was wondering – how did he die exactly? If you don't mind me asking?"

"It's kind of you to think of Arthur, Mr Harrison," Miss Richards said, pursing her lips. "It was a sad end for such a fine lad, but a heroic one. He saved the lives of many other men."

"How exactly?" Charlie was desperate to get to his room and bathe his stinging skin in cold water, but his feet were rooted to the stairs. He had to know. He had to have his suspicions confirmed, despite the churning in his guts warning him not to dig any deeper.

"It was a mustard gas attack in the trenches last December," Miss Richards told him. "The Germans were throwing everything they had at our boys, including those awful chemicals they put in their shells. There were so many coming at them, Arthur's trench was saturated with the stuff. It isn't really a gas, you know," she said, her voice quavering, "it's a vapour. It hangs in the air, soaking into the soldiers' skin, and then it pools in the mud. The only way to escape it is to climb to higher ground. That's what

Arthur did – he made sure the rest of the boys were safely up on higher ground before he tried to get out himself. But he slipped and fell in a pool of the stuff, and –"

Miss Richards broke off with a choked sob.

Charlie remembered the dream, remembered looking back from halfway up a ladder at the boy floundering in the mud, reaching a hand up to him for help.

"I'm very sorry to hear that, Miss Richards," he said. "I hope he didn't suffer long."

"Don't you remember what that stuff does?" Miss Richards looked up at him, her expression pained. Before he could think of an answer she said, "He lingered on for weeks! He was soaked from head to toe in it, and by the time they got him to a field hospital his skin was red raw and peeling off in strips. When they got him home to England he was so badly blistered and covered in bandages his mother didn't even recognise him. Not that he would have recognised her either by then, what with the horrible state his poor eyes were in..."

Charlie didn't push her any further. He didn't need to imagine how the boy had looked. He was sure by now he'd already seen the damage up close.

"It was almost a relief when he passed, with all he was suffering," Miss Richards went on without further prompting, eager now to relieve her aching heart by sharing her burden. "Not that his mother saw it that way. When he died on Christmas Eve I could almost hear her heart breaking. She didn't last more than a day after that."

"She died of a broken heart?" Charlie's eyebrows shot up. He thought that only happened in cheap penny romances.

"Of course not! She took a draught to end her own suffering." Miss Richards looked around as though fearing the walls were listening and then whispered, "Opium, it was. The Doctor had given it to her to calm her nerves. It wasn't his fault of course, but I know he still feels terrible about it. That's why I was so reluctant to take you in over Christmas at first, what with it being the one-year anniversary and everything, but now I think I'll be glad of the company."

She gave him a sad little smile, and Charlie tried to smile back, but his face was still stinging and his hands were so sore it came out as a grimace.

"I'll fetch you some antiseptic liquid for your cuts, and some bandages," Miss Richards said again, hurrying off to her medicine cabinet. This time Charlie didn't object. With his shredded nerves and fear that the apparition might reappear to haunt his dreams, he was glad of the company too.

* * * * * *

That night, as he lay on the narrow guest room bed with his hands in bandages and his precious book tucked under his pillow for safe-keeping, the dream returned.

Clamping his hands over his ears to drown out the sharp crack of exploding shells and the screams of dying men, Charlie stumbled through the trench, seeking the soldier whose face was haunting his waking hours. This time when the cry of 'GAS!'

came and the young man from the photo pushed him towards the ladder, he knew what to do.

Instead of climbing the ladder to escape the gas and leaving the soldier to flounder in the mud, Charlie choked back his fear along with great lungfuls of the gas and turned back when the young man fell.

"Help me!" Arthur cried, wet mud slipping though his fingers as he tried to pull himself up. "Help!"

"Grab my hand!" Charlie shouted, leaning as far over the toxic pool as he dared. "Hurry!"

"I can't reach!" Arthur coughed. "Closer! Come closer!"

Charlie edged forward, his boots sinking in the mud. He could feel the liquid seeping through the leather and soaking his socks. He wouldn't feel the burning straight away. Mustard gas did its gruesome work slowly and stealthily, and by the time serious exposure was detected, it was usually too late to stop the damage.

"Take my hand!" Charlie yelled again. "I'll pull you out."

Arthur's fingers were just inches from his, when Charlie felt his whole weight shift. His hands drooped heavily, and when he looked down, he saw the rings from countless burglaries sparkling in the flaring light. Diamond bracelets, the treasure from every society belle he'd ever robbed, snaked round his wrists like bands of steel. He staggered, trying to regain his balance, but his coat and trouser pockets were weighed down by watch chains and sovereigns, snuff-boxes and cigarette cases. Every trinket he'd ever stolen was now conspiring to send him toppling to his doom.

"No! I'm trying to help! I'm trying to do the right thing!" Charlie whimpered, tottering on the edge of the deadly pool. All it would take was one more small weight, and he'd lose his balance in the mud.

"Help me!" Charlie pleaded, locking eyes with the young man reaching up to him from the pool. "Help!"

Arthur's eyes were red and bloodshot, the colour of poppies dying at sunset. His voice came out in a choked hiss, his throat raw with pain.

"Remember me!" he gasped. *"Remember!"*

Charlie felt a final weight added to his pocket, and he looked down to find *The Art of War* poking out of his stolen coat. That was the last thing he saw before he toppled towards the pool, screaming in terror until the polluted waters closed over his head and drowned his cry.

* * * * * *

The acrid smell of mustard gas and the cloying scent of dying poppies followed him all the way to the Bookshop the following afternoon. Charlie cupped his bandaged hands against a window and peered into its dark depths, searching for signs of life. Nothing stirred in the gloom. Even the dust was silent in the grey winter light slanting in from outside. This time the sign on the door announced, 'Closed until January 6th', and nothing in the silence of the Bookshop contradicted its claim.

Charlie hesitated on the step, weighing his options.

His nerves were in shreds, and it had taken all of his strength to drag himself out of bed in time for a late luncheon at the guest house. Miss Richards had pursed her lips and served him sandwiches without referring to his non-appearance at breakfast, but she was growing suspicious of him, he could tell. It didn't help that she'd caught him rummaging through the kitchen drawers last night looking for something to pawn. That had taken some explaining, and no mistake.

He needed to get some money today, or he wouldn't be able to pay his bill for the next few nights, never mind a train ticket to London. He wanted to get back to the City so badly he could almost smell his own desperation through the stench of mustard and the sickly sweet scent of poppy that seemed to follow him everywhere now. His hands were too sore and blistered to pickpocket his way through the busy shops in broad daylight, and with the heavy bandages restricting his fingers, he'd never get away with it anyway.

He'd been all out of ideas until Miss Richards suggested he spend the afternoon at the Electric

Theatre on Chapel Street. Charlie suspected she was just trying to get him out of the house so she could do her Christmas shopping without worrying about him making off with her cutlery, but it was the perfect solution to his problems. A trip to the dark theatre, with patrons too occupied by a film to notice his wandering hands, however clumsy they might be at the moment, would fund his ticket back to civilisation and safety.

It was only when he'd crossed The Square and passed the Bookshop, that another idea had distracted him for just a moment.

Don't be such a fool! Charlie told himself, shaking his head to clear the mad thought that flashed through his brain at the sight of the Bookshop signboard. *It's my book. Mine! I'm not giving it up now!*

Fortunately, the Bookshop was shut up, and his lock picks were stolen, or the warning voice whispering in his ear might have got its own way and made him return his treasure to the counter where he'd found it.

A few bad dreams and you go soft, is that it, Charlie Briggs? he chided himself. *Pull yourself together and get back on the job!*

The Art of War weighed heavily in his jacket pocket, but it was there to stay until Charlie could get it to Keeler. He shoved his aching hands into his pockets and turned into Chapel Street, squinting at the shop fronts he passed to find the Electric Theatre. His eyes were stinging so badly he could barely make out the words on the signs above him, but it was his feet that were worrying him most. His eyes he could explain. They were irritated by the strange smoke in the Spain Arms. And his hands? Well, the smoke could have got to them too, he hadn't been wearing gloves after all. That could also explain why his face was red and peeling today. He couldn't have stood the pain of shaving even if his razor hadn't been stolen.

But his feet..?

He'd woken up to find his toes and ankles swollen and blisters bursting on his soles as he got out of bed. His skin was raw and cracked, and pulling on his socks and boots had been torture. He daren't call for a doctor, though. The fewer people he talked to here, the safer his secret would be. Keeler would sort him out with medical care when he got back to London. All he had to do was get through the next few days and it would all be over.

The sign for the Electric Theatre swam into focus up ahead. Charlie dug a hand into his pocket and pulled out the last of his coins, paying for a ticket at the counter and hurrying inside.

The film was nearly over when he chose a mark to sit next to near the back of the stalls. The theatre was busy today, full of people trying to escape the cold and find a little Christmas cheer. A crowd-pleasing Chaplin film was showing, and the audience howled with laughter as the little tramp waddled across the screen twirling his walking stick, oblivious to the carnage he was leaving in his wake.

Charlie shuffled a little closer to the man sitting next to him, his hand snaking out to feel inside his coat pocket. It was the wrong crowd for silver cigarette cases and inlaid snuff-boxes, but if he was lucky he might find a labourer's Christmas bonus or turkey savings ready for a call at the butchers. Hampered by the bandages Miss Richards had wound round his hands, Charlie's fingers were heavy and clumsy, and it was slow work getting them inside.

"He's a right laugh, him, isn't he?" The man suddenly twisted in his seat to face Charlie, and his coat moved, trapping Charlie's swollen hand in its folds It wasn't a young labourer like Charlie thought. This man was much older, and in the darkness Charlie could just make out the scars on the other side of his face. He'd seen many soldiers return from the Front with shell damage just like it.

He nodded weakly, suddenly ashamed of himself without knowing why. He'd robbed more War veterans than he could count without feeling the slightest twinge of guilt before now. With their wooden legs and shaky nerves, they'd never been able to follow him or shout for help before he'd vanished into the crowd. Today it felt different, though. For the first time ever, it felt wrong.

But was too late to back out now. Charlie's fingers had already closed over the coins in the man's pocket, and when he turned back to the screen again, Charlie drew his hand out slowly, careful not to get his thick bandages caught and raise the alarm. When his hand was safely back in his own lap he examined each coin in the dark with his fingertips. Even through the blisters and the swelling, his experience told him the exact value of the money in his grasp.

One shilling and five pence.

Barely enough for a few pints and a meal at a cheap pub, never mind a train ticket home. He'd just robbed a war hero of his Christmas dinner for nothing. If the rest of the men in the crowd were as poor as he was, Charlie would have to rob dozens of them to pay for his bed and board and his way out of Petersfield.

His stomach turned at the thought.

Or maybe it was the smell that was making him queasy. The darkness was heavy with the bitter tang of mustard which seemed to grow stronger with each passing moment. He rubbed his stinging eyes with his bandaged hands, trying to work out if the yellow cloud hovering in the flickering light was really there or just in his imagination. For a moment the screen dimmed, the piano music ending on a jarring chord that set his teeth on edge.

When the picture reappeared, Charlie's heart skipped a beat at what he saw playing out on the screen. It was a scene straight from hell, one he recognised only too well despite the yellow haze that clouded his vision. The Chaplin film had been replaced with an image from his nightmare, and the sound of shell-fire filled his head with an awful roar. It was as though the camera had captured everything he saw in his dreams: the dying soldiers, the blood-splattered walls of the trenches, and even the mud that sucked at his feet in the darkness.

Another shell exploded and three men turned to blood and bone and uniform shreds. The audience roared with laughter, clapping and hooting as more shells whistled overhead, throwing up mud as they detonated. Charlie tried to get up and run, but it was almost as though the seats around him had turned to mud too, and his hands slipped off their slick surfaces, unable to find purchase.

Then a voice, high-pitched with terror, cried out above the noise.

"Gas!" it screamed. "*GAS!*"

Suddenly the laughter of the audience died and silence filled the theatre, broken only by Charlie's hacking coughs. He covered his mouth with his sleeve, but the choking smell got worse and worse until he could barely breathe.

"We have to get out!" he yelled at the man next to him, the one he'd robbed only moments before. The old soldier turned to look at him in the darkness, but in place of his face, now there was only a gas mask with black holes for eyes.

"Good God" Charlie lurched to his feet and stumbled back. Every head in the theatre turned towards him, dozens and dozens of gas masks gazing blindly at him through the sulphurous fog.

"Help me!"

Charlie wasn't sure if it was his own voice he heard calling out, or the voice of the man whose familiar face filled the screen. A young soldier was floundering in the mud, trying to drag himself out the mire trapping him at the bottom of the trench.

"Help me!" Arthur called again, reaching out his hand for him. Charlie hesitated in the aisle one second too long. The soldier fell back, exhausted by his efforts, the mustard vapour burning its way over every inch of exposed skin.

"Remember me!"

Charlie whirled round. Every hand in the theatre was raised towards him, red eyes blazing through the black hollows of gas masks. Before the ghostly figures could surge towards him, Charlie fled, crashing back through the doors and galloping down Chapel Street as fast as his blistered feet could carry him.

Only one thought was clear in his frantic mind as he made for the Post Office in Levant Street: no matter how fast he ran, he'd never be able to escape the stench of mustard and the haunting scent of poppies.

* * * * * *

"I'm telling you, Keeler, you have to come and get me out of here!" Charlie shouted down the Post Office telephone. "It just isn't safe!"

"Calm down, Charlie Boy," Keeler's soothing voice oozed honey through the receiver. "Just another few weeks or so and the heat'll be off here. Once you get back and I have that book, we can –"

"You're not listening to me!" Charlie yelled, attracting the frowns of the post master and the curious stares of the customers queuing with their letters and Christmas parcels. He lowered his voice and hissed, "I'm out of money! I told you I can't do another job here – my hands can't take it. If you want this book you'll have to come down and get me tomorrow."

"Come on, Charlie, you know that's not possible," Keeler said. "I've got too many eyes on me, and I can't be seen with you right now."

"You either come and get me, or God help me, I'm selling this book to Dixon the minute I find a way out of this hell-hole," Charlie spat. He'd never threatened Keeler before, it was a dangerous thing to do to such a well-connected dealer. But Charlie was out of options. He had to get out of here somehow, and he was too ill to walk far and too badly blistered to steal his fare. Keeler was his only way out.

"Fine," Keeler snapped, the honeyed tone replaced by a hard edge. "I'll get my cousin Jim to drive us down in his car. But it'll have to be Boxing Day, Charlie, I can't make it before then."

"But–"

"No arguments! I'm sticking my neck out for you, and that book better be worth it. It's in perfect condition, right?"

"Yes, it's perfect," Charlie growled, "which is more than I can say for this arrangement. I need out *now*, Keeler, not in three days' time!"

"It's the best I can do, Charlie. Take it or leave it."

Charlie knew how badly Keeler wanted the book. If he was giving Charlie an ultimatum then it meant he couldn't do any better.

"Alright," he sighed, rubbing his sore eyes. "Three days, and not a moment later."

"Meet us at the train station at noon on Boxing Day. I've put some feelers out, and that book's going to make our fortune, Charlie Boy, just you wait and see."

Sickened by the gloating note in Keeler's voice, Charlie muttered a goodbye and hung up. Three more days stuck in Petersfield. How the hell was he going to stop himself going completely round the bend before Boxing Day?

He paid for the call with the pilfered theatre coins, trying to erase the awful images in his head as he stepped back out into the cold. Darkness had closed in while he made his call, and the lamplighter was making his rounds. The shops had already shut up, and their owners and customers had returned to their warm fires and hearty dinners. Charlie was alone on the corner of Levant Street and Chapel Street, trying to decide what to do next.

He didn't relish passing the Electric Theatre again, but nor did he want to risk getting lost in the gloom trying to find a different route. He remembered only too well the strange figure that had followed him down Sheep Street from the Spain Arms, and around the Heath Pond in the fog. Tonight he'd follow the light of the gas lamps, and return to the guest house by the quickest route. He headed back into Chapel Street, turning his thin collar up against the cold and hiding his burning hands in his pockets.

His boots felt heavy on his blistered feet, and before long he was limping, shifting his weight from leg to leg to keep the pressure off his swollen toes. The darkness seemed to be spreading as he made his way down Chapel Street, the pale light from the gas lamps barely illuminating the frost-covered pavement. Charlie shivered and stumbled on faster, feeling every hair on the back of his neck prickling as he reached the Electric Theatre. Lamps glowed in its windows, like a lighthouse warning of ghost ships.

Straining his bleary eyes, Charlie was relieved to see there was nothing more unusual inside than a bored-looking man at the ticket booth and a few patrons chatting in the lobby. No gas masks. No hands reaching out in the dark. Nothing to be frightened of.

Yet somehow Charlie couldn't shake the chill that closed around his bones and bit deep. His fear took shape, manifesting as a yellow fog that rolled in from the narrow alleyways and enveloped the gaslights. He'd seen that fog before, and he knew what it meant. He forced his aching feet on faster, fighting the urge to look over his shoulder.

The smell of death was back, hanging heavy on the frosty air and seeping into his lungs like poison. His skin felt like it was on fire, and his trembling hands scratched at his neck, trying to ease the itch that was spreading up to his face. Before he could reach the faint glow of the next streetlight, his foot caught on a loose flagstone in the dark and he tripped, falling to the ground and hitting his knee hard against the pavement.

Damn it! Charlie cursed, grabbing the lamppost and pulling himself up. As he did so, he couldn't avoid glancing back down Chapel Street.

A figure was standing in the doorway of the Electric Theatre.

When it turned towards him, Charlie felt a finger of ice run up his spine. In the gloom he could make out no features, just a misshapen lump of a gas mask for a face, and the tattered ends of bandages flapping in the breeze.

Then it began to move.

Slowly at first, then faster and faster. It came hobbling down Chapel Street towards him, its red eyes shining eerily through the fog. Charlie tried to run, but with his blistered feet and aching knee he could do no more than stumble blindly down the road, the pale glow of the streetlights his only guide in the night.

The bitter smell of mustard was intense, and he coughed and spluttered as he turned the corner into The Square, grasping the windowsill of the Bookshop to stop himself from falling as he fought for breath. The silence of the Bookshop seemed to mock him now as the shuffling footfalls behind him grew louder.

If I just had my lock picks I could get inside and replace this damn book before it –

There was no time for regrets, and no way now to atone for his crime. All Charlie could do was try to make it to safety before the thing in the fog caught him.

He limped across The Square, making for the looming statue of the horse and rider that guarded the crossroads. Apart from the metal King and his mount, The Square was strangely empty. The yellow fog was so thick now, Charlie couldn't even see the welcoming lights of the George Inn or the spire of the church up ahead. Somewhere off to his left he could just make out the muffled sound of music and laughter from the Corn Exchange where a pre-Christmas dance was being held, but the old building seemed so distant, so far out of reach, it might as well only exist in a dream. After his experience in the Electric Theatre, Charlie knew he was no safer in a crowd.

He had to get back to the guest house, it was the only place he could hide from the monster in the dark.

The footfalls behind him were edging closer as he finally turned down St Peter's Road. His knee was aching so badly he had slowed to a crawl. The thing was gaining on him with every step.

Don't look back! he told himself. *Whatever you do, Charlie Briggs, don't look back!*

Every nerve was strained to breaking point as he stumbled along the pavement, and he couldn't help it, he just had to *know*.

Charlie looked back.

The figure was right behind him, its ghostly hands reaching out for him. The sinister red eyes burned brightly in the darkness, yellow mist seeping from the gas mask with each hissing breath.

"Remember me!" a voice seemed to echo in the darkness as it loomed over him. *"Remember!"*

Charlie choked back a sob of fear and grabbed the iron railings skirting the houses, puling himself along with hands that screamed in pain. He scrabbled at the gate to the guesthouse, fumbling the latch with his blistered fingers and tripping up the steps.

"Let me in!" he cried, pounding at the door so hard his knuckles bled. "For the love of God, LET ME IN!"

The skin on the back of his neck burned painfully as a bandaged hand came creeping out of the dark to grasp at him, a cloud of mustard gas enveloping Charlie in its scalding vapours.

"NO! It's not my fault! PLEASE DON'T –"

"Mr Harrison! What on earth..?"

The door was opened so suddenly Charlie tumbled headfirst onto the mat in the hall. He lay there stunned for a long moment, coughing and spluttering as the yellow fog began to clear and he could breathe again.

"Is everything alright? Are you unwell?"

Charlie squinted up at the old lady who was frowning down at him. He followed her gaze to the street as she peered into the darkness, trying to work out what could have caused such a commotion. The night was crisp and clear, the streetlamps burning brightly against the inky sky. There was no fog, and no ghostly figure waiting to claim him.

"Mr Harrison, have you been drinking?"

Charlie threw his head back and laughed, a grim, hysterical sound that echoed all the way down the street to the silent graveyard circling the church.

* * * * * *

"You're sure you don't want to come to the carol service tonight?" Miss Richards asked for what seemed like the hundredth time. "You haven't been out of the house all day, Mr Harrison. A breath of fresh air and some lovely Christmas Eve hymns might do you good."

"No thank you, Miss Richards," Charlie called back through his locked bedroom door. "I'm very tired. I'd like to turn in early."

"If you're sure..."

Charlie bit back his irritation when he heard the old lady hovering on the landing outside his door. He knew she wanted company tonight, on the anniversary of her nephew's death, but she'd be better off finding comfort in her friends from church, rather than a stranger at her guest house.

When Miss Richards' footsteps faded down the stairs and the front door closed behind her, Charlie breathed a sigh of relief and stretched out on the bed. He hadn't slept a wink last night, and he'd no intention of sleeping tonight either, even if his fevered brain was capable of switching off long enough to allow him to rest. He couldn't face the dream again. He couldn't bear to see those tortured eyes gazing up at him in false hope, begging to be saved. Besides, his whole body was so swollen and blistered by now, he wouldn't be able to sleep with the itching pain even if he wanted to.

He winced as he shifted on the bed, sores along his back breaking painfully as he reached for the book on the nightstand. All he had to do was get through another two nights without sleep, and the cavalry in the shape of Keeler would arrive to take him back home. This little volume would be sold to the highest bidder, and his days of hustling for money would be a distant memory, along with the nightmares that haunted him.

He stroked the cover lovingly with his aching fingers, forcing himself to think about the good life to come, the life he was *owed*. He might not have fought in the War, but hadn't he done his time too? Hadn't he had his own trenches to crawl through, in the basements and backstairs of London? Hadn't he got his fair share of War wounds to show for his troubles? This was *his* War trophy, and he'd be damned if some hallucination caused by the Spain Arms thieves was going to rob him of his reward. His book was beautiful. His book was perfect.

Charlie opened the front cover and gazed at the yellow pages in dismay.

His book was *damaged!*

The paper was blistered and cracked, as though the book had been soaked in an acid solution and then left to dry in the sun.

"That's not possible!" he howled in dismay. *It was perfect just a few minutes ago!*

He turned the pages in growing desperation. Every leaf was mottled and warped, the binding coming apart in Charlie's own damaged hands.

"How?" Charlie gasped. *How did this happen?*

Maybe this was another hallucination, another waking dream caused by the after-effects of the Spain Arms sedative. Maybe all he had to do was go to sleep, and in the morning he'd find *The Art of War* in perfect condition again, and his greed repaid in full.

Or maybe this was Arthur's revenge for the theft of his book from its rightful owner. Maybe he'd return this Christmas Eve, on the anniversary of his death, to claim it.

Charlie hugged the blackened book to his burning chest, his mind whirling.

It can't come inside, the thing I saw, he told himself. *It lives in the shadows and the fog. It can't reach me here. As long as I stay inside until Boxing Day, I'll be safe.*

The thought reassured him, until he remembered something that made his heart almost stop dead.

This was Arthur's house, he thought. *He lived here!*

And maybe, though Miss Richards hadn't made it clear where it had happened, just maybe he had died here too.

He wasn't any safer in this house than he was out in the dark street.

Suddenly the light in the bedroom flickered, the gas lamps dimming until only the faint glow from the dying fire was left to throw shadows across the walls. The coals hissed and popped in the grate, a faint yellow smoke rising as they resettled. The air filled with the sharp tang of mustard and the sickly smell of withered flowers, and Charlie knew with dreadful certainty what he would see if he stayed in this locked room one moment longer.

He leapt from his bed to grab his jacket from the chair in the corner, and came face to face with the figure standing just inches away from him.

Charlie stumbled back with a cry, his eyes wide with shock at the sight of the gas mask leering down at him, and the bandaged hands that came groping for his neck in the gloom. He grabbed the blackened book from the bed and threw himself at the door, sliding back the bolt and crashing down the stairs three at a time.

The house was horribly dark, the tiny flames of the gas lamps hissing and spluttering away to nothing as he passed. He could hear heavy footfalls on the floorboards above, and choking yellow gas began to roll down towards him from the landing. For one mad moment he hesitated at the door to the dining room, the stolen book weighing heavily in his blistered hands.

Should I put it back on the bookshelf with the rest of the collection? he thought desperately. *Would it all go away if I just returned it?*

But this house wasn't where the book belonged. Arthur's mother hadn't wanted it kept here. Miss Richards had given it away. It belonged in the Bookshop with Doctor Roberts.

The footsteps thudded through the ice-cold fog, following him into the hall. Charlie had no more time to waste. He stumbled down the front steps without bothering to close the door behind him, limping down St Peter's Road and praying he'd make it to the Bookshop in time. The fog closed in around him, the muffled footsteps behind him spurring him on despite his aching body and stinging eyes. He clutched at the railings, using them half for support to stop his trembling legs from giving way, and half to drag himself forward.

By the time he reached The Square, the fog was so thick he couldn't make out a single landmark in the yellow haze. He whirled this way and that, stumbling blindly in the dark, trying to find the statue of King William III and his horse to guide him. He had to find the Bookshop. He'd leave the book on the front step for Doctor Roberts to find, and maybe, just *maybe,* that would be enough to stop the monster that hunted him.

He groped in the dark with fingers that screamed in pain each time he moved them. Reaching out, they found something in the fog. It wasn't the cold lead of the statue or the hard marble of its plinth. His fingers sank into something soft and fleshy, like a seeping wound half covered with dressings. Red eyes burned far brighter than the pale streetlamps, barring his path and forcing him to back away.

"What do you want?" Charlie cried, his voice swallowed up by the fog almost as soon as the words left his lips. "Why are you following me?

The only answer was a hiss of gas escaping from a mask and the awful shuffling sound of footsteps coming nearer.

Then he heard it. Another sound that made his heart leap in hope.

Singing.

Voices called faintly in the night, the carol they sang a welcome beacon to guide him to the safety of the church. Charlie willed his burning feet on, following the sound of the choir across The Square until he came to the door of St Peter's church. It was open, welcoming all those who sought refuge from the bitter cold. He stifled a sob of relief as he limped inside, the flickering candles lighting his way to an empty back pew where he almost collapsed in exhaustion.

It's over, he gasped, sucking down the fresh, untainted air greedily. *It can't touch me in here.*

Charlie didn't have much experience of churches, but he knew they were no place for the damned. He was too tired to work out whether that included him or not. He set the stolen book down on the shelf before him, as desperate now to rid himself of it as he had once been to obtain it.

Maybe if I leave it here, one of the congregation will return it to its rightful owner and I'll finally be free, he thought, picking up a hymn book instead and struggling to turn the pages with his scorched fingers. The organ music swelled, the choir and the congregation joining their voices for the chorus of 'God Rest Ye Merry Gentlemen.' Charlie looked down at his hymn book and let out a cry of dismay.

The pages were blackened and bubbled, just like *The Art of War*.

Everything he touched was blighted with his corruption. There was no place left for him to hide.

As the song ended and the minister ascended his pulpit once more, the flickering candles burned brighter and sweeter, their odour no longer one of hot wax, but of red poppy fields trampled to mud. One by one they began to blink out, black smoke trailing in the darkness they left behind. The minister waited until the last strains of the carol had died away, then he opened his mouth, uttering the word Charlie had hoped never to hear again as long as he lived.

"Gas!" he cried. *"GAS!"*

As one, every head in the church turned to face Charlie. Every man, woman and child in the pews and every white-gowned chorister in the stalls was gone, replaced by ghostly figures of long-dead soldiers with gas masks for faces and burning red hollows for eyes.

Charlie staggered to his feet and fled for the side door, knocking over flower stands full of dying poppies and crashing into a font frothing with sulphurous vapour. Choking, burning, limping and flailing, he stumbled into the cemetery, tripping over tombstones that reared out of the yellow fog circling the church. There was nowhere left for him to go, nowhere left to hide from his sins.

His legs gave out, and he fell next to the statue of an angel whose eyes wept blood as they gazed down at him. He scrabbled at the ground, trying to pull himself forward, away from the awful shuffling footsteps that followed him through the night. But his strength was gone, and he collapsed, rolling over on the cold stone to face the figure in the mask who loomed over him.

"Is this what you've come for? Here, take it! I don't want it anymore!" he sobbed, thrusting the book towards the outstretched hands. But the blackened cover of this book had once been blue, not brown. It was a hymn book from the church he was holding, not the stolen volume from the Bookshop. The red eyes in the mask burned brighter as the searching hands found Charlie's neck. Two bandaged claws closed around his throat, and Charlie felt his whole body burn with the heat of a thousand coals. He screamed and thrashed, just as the dying man in the trenches had done, but it was equally useless. His fate was sealed.

"What do you want?" he choked again, his vision dimming until all he could see was the glowing eyes that looked like two poppies set alight at dusk.

"Remember me!" the voice hissed. *"Remember!"*

Suddenly Charlie was no longer in the cemetery, but back in the trenches, stumbling through the mud as shells exploded all around. His feet slipped before he could find the ladder, and he went tumbling down, down into an icy pool that burned with cold fire.

"Help me!" he cried, reaching out to the soldier who was climbing the ladder to safety above him. "Help!"

The man turned, and just for the briefest moment, Charlie found himself staring into his own eyes. Then the man was gone, leaving Charlie alone in the dark waters that closed over his head.

There was no one left to hear him scream.

* * * * * *

"A bad business," the minister shook his head, watching the policemen lift the body wrapped in a blanket onto a stretcher. "A sad start to this day of peace."

"The poor man's at peace now," Doctor Roberts said, "whoever he was."

"Is there no one who can identify him?"

"His face is too badly burned, and as for the rest of him... well, the less said about that the better," the Doctor shuddered.

"Were there no clues left with the body? No belongings that could help us find his family?"

"Nothing but a charred book. I've no idea which one, the pages are utterly destroyed. But talking of books, the verger handed this to me this morning – he said it was left on one of the pews." Doctor Roberts opened his bag and took out a handsome volume covered in marbled brown leather.

"One of yours, is it?" the minister asked.

"Yes, but goodness knows how it got there," Doctor Roberts frowned, leafing through the pages of *The Art of War*. The precious volume was thankfully intact, the pages crisp and clean. "Last time I saw it, it was headed for my safe. Which makes me wonder..." He frowned, gazing after the shrouded figure on the stretcher as the policemen made their slow way through the gravestones.

"You wondered..?" the minister prompted.

"Nothing. Never mind. Let's get out of the cold. It's Christmas Day after all, and I could do with something hot to drink."

"Come along to the manse, the police will be joining us there shortly," the minister agreed.

As they walked through the graveyard, their feet crunching on the frost-covered grass, Doctor Roberts drew in a deep breath of the sharp winter air. Something seemed to linger in the breeze, a faint, but familiar scent, full of memories and half-remembered dreams. Doctor Roberts turned, looking back at the spot where the scorched body had been found.

There, growing through the hard ground by the statue of an angel, was a single red poppy that swayed and danced in the wind.

Victoria Williamson is a children's author who grew up in Kirkintilloch, north Glasgow, surrounded by hills, books, and an historic farm estate which inspired many of her early adventure stories and spooky tales. After studying Physics at the University of Glasgow, she set out on her own real-life adventures, which included teaching maths and science in Cameroon, training teachers in Malawi, teaching English in China and working with children with additional support needs in the UK.

A qualified primary school teacher with a degree in Mandarin Chinese from Yunnan University and an MA in Special Needs in Education, Victoria is passionate about creating inclusive worlds in her children's novels where all youngsters can see a reflection of themselves in a heroic role. Victoria has a deep interest in history and archaeology, and her debut adult novella combines her love of exploring the past with her fascination with supernatural tales.

Victoria divides her time between writing, visiting schools and literary festivals to discuss books and reading, and running creative writing classes.

IT'S ALWAYS MIDNIGHT SOMEWHERE

ISBN: 978-1-3999-3887-7

All things have patterns, if you're willing to look hard enough...

May Snow is a supernatural cartographer, a pattern-finder, a draughtswoman of the unfathomable. Some say she's a living ghost.

When May sets out to trace the origins and path of the elusive Midnight Train, it proves far more difficult to unravel than any dark magic she has previously encountered. Fellow passenger Kara seems to know more than she's letting on and why does she seem familiar? Who or what is the heartbeat of the train? Is it sentient or mere machinery? What are the passengers searching for... or running from?

Dictating her findings into her trusty tape recorder, May discovers how her own destiny is stitched into the fabric of the Midnight Train, and that this adventure could be her last.